Brave Little Raccoon

To Allen +
Ousu,
Be brave in everything
you do! Enjoy,
xoxo
Erica Wolf

Written and Illustrated by
Erica Wolf

Henry Holt and Company

New York

Henry Holt and Company, LLC
Publishers since 1866
115 West 18th Street
New York, New York 10011
www.henryholt.com

Henry Holt is a registered trademark of Henry Holt and Company, LLC
Copyright © 2005 by Erica Wolf
Distributed in Canada by H. B. Fenn and Company Ltd.

Library of Congress Cataloging-in-Publication Data
Wolf, Erica.
Brave little raccoon / Erica Wolf.—1st ed.
p.   cm.
Summary: When Little Raccoon wanders off one day, she finds herself on her own,
with all kinds of strange noises around her.
ISBN-13: 978-0-8050-7408-6
ISBN-10: 0-8050-7408-2
[1. Raccoons—Fiction. 2. Mother and child—Fiction. 3. Fear—Fiction.] I. Title.
PZ7.W8185517Br 2005   [E]—dc22   2004008981

First Edition—2005 / Designed by Patrick Collins
The artist used acrylics on Rives BFK paper to create the illustrations for this book.
Printed in the United States of America on acid-free paper. ∞

10 9 8 7 6 5 4 3 2 1

For my niece, Katelyn,
who should always listen
to her mother
— Love, Erica

Fall had arrived, and Little Raccoon left her den to chase the leaves that danced in the wind. She heard a CHATTER, CHATTER and knew that her mother had followed her.

"Now don't wander off too far," Mother told Little Raccoon. "It's getting late, and you're still too young to be out alone in the dark."

Little Raccoon followed
a bright yellow leaf on
its long journey past
the meadow . . .

and through the forest . . .

. . . until it landed softly in a stream.
    She was having such a good time that she
forgot what her mother had told her.

Little Raccoon chased after the yellow leaf
as it floated downstream.
    The daylight soon faded. Little Raccoon
would have to find her way home in the
dark all by herself.

As the sounds of night began to emerge,
the familiar forest became strange and scary.
Little Raccoon felt very little.

Still, she worked up enough courage to begin
her walk toward home.
Before she got far, there was a loud SNAP, SNAP
in the distance. Little Raccoon scurried along.

SNAP, SNAP! There was that noise again, and it sounded closer. Little Raccoon looked around quickly and headed for the cattails near the stream. She tried to be extra brave.

But when Little Raccoon poked her head into the cattails, she found a great big bullfrog sitting among them.

The bullfrog let out a loud CROAK. Little Raccoon was so surprised she bounded out

SNAP, SNAP! RUSTLE, RUSTLE! Something was still following Little Raccoon! She saw a hollow log and decided to hide inside it.

But when Little Raccoon crawled
into the log, she discovered a
family of opossums.
There wasn't much
room left for her, so she
continued on her way.

Little Raccoon began to trot. She missed her mother and wanted to find her home.

SNAP, SNAP! RUSTLE, RUSTLE! Whatever was
following Little Raccoon was getting close!
She quickly climbed up the nearest tree.

But when Little Raccoon reached the branches, she saw a large owl perched up high. The owl gave a HOOT, which startled her, and she scampered back down to the ground, heading toward the meadow.

By now she was running as fast as her legs would take her. RUSTLE, RUSTLE! The sound was right behind Little Raccoon.
She needed a place to hide—and quick!

Little Raccoon dove into a pile of leaves.
She sat very still and tried not to rustle
the brush around her.
Just then she heard a familiar sound.
CHATTER, CHATTER! Could it be . . . ?

Yes! It was her mother! She had been following Little Raccoon's tracks all night long.

"I'm so glad you are safe, Little Raccoon. You were very brave, but please don't wander off on your own again."

They started back together toward
their den. Little Raccoon was glad to be
by her mother's side. She had tried her
best to be brave and didn't feel quite so
little anymore.

Now whenever Little Raccoon sees
a bright yellow leaf dancing in the
wind, she still chases it, but not too
far from home.